Take a Breath Olive Tran

Library and Archives Canada Cataloguing in Publication

Title: Take a breath Olive Tran / written by Phuong Truong ; illustrations by Christine Wei.
Names: Truong, Phuong, author. | Wei, Christine, illustrator.
Description: Series statement: Olive Tran series ; 2 | Text chiefly in English; some text in Vietnamese.
Identifiers: Canadiana (print) 20250145154 | Canadiana (ebook) 20250148218 | ISBN 9781772604276 (softcover) | ISBN 9781772604283 (EPUB)
Subjects: LCGFT: Novels.
Classification: LCC PS8639.R86 T35 2025 | DDC jC813/.6—dc23

Copyright © 2025 Phuong Truong
Cover and illustrations by Christine Wei
Printed and bound in Canada

Second Story Press gratefully acknowledges the support of the Ontario Arts Council and the Canada Council for the Arts for our publishing program. We acknowledge the financial support of the Government of Canada through the Canada Book Fund.

Second Story Press expressly prohibits the use of *Take a Breath Olive Tran* in connection with the development of any software program, including, without limitation, training a machine learning or generative artificial intelligence (AI) system.

Published by
SECOND STORY PRESS
120 Carlton Street, Suite 412
Toronto, ON, M5A 4K2
www.secondstorypress.ca

Take a Breath Olive Tran

Second Story Press

Written by
Phuong Truong

Illustrations by
Christine Wei

Chapter 1

Now that I am officially ten years old—ahem, the first in my class, no less—it's time to get serious. We're almost halfway through the school year, and so far, it's been good. But as the oldest student in my class, it's my job, my *duty*, to make this the *Best. Year. Ever.*

Every year, Maple Avenue Elementary has a mid-year talent show, which the teachers think helps the students get past the halfway slump. They're not wrong.

Take a Breath Olive Tran

Besides being treated as celebrities for the rest of the year, the best act, as chosen by the students, wins a pizza party for their class. My friends might as well place their orders now, 'cause that party is as good as ours. My notebook is open, my pen at the ready. All I need is a little inspiration.

"Yo, space cadet!" My brother, Ben, waves his hand in front of my face. "I asked if you were gonna eat that."

I do some of my best thinking at our kitchen table, surrounded by goodies. Unfortunately, it's not the most private place to work. I swat at Ben's hand as I slide the plate holding the last custard bun toward him. "I was thinking!"

"Oof, don't hurt yourself." Before I can reclaim my snack, Ben crams half of it in

2

Phuong Truong

his mouth. How do boys eat so much so quickly? "What's got you all worked up?" he asks around a mouthful of bun. Gross.

"I'm just thinking about the talent show." I sigh and get up to fetch a glass of water. Mom says I get enough sugar from the Kandy Korner, our local convenience store, so our home has a strict no juice, no soda policy. All we have is milk, water, and a million different types of tea.

"Ah yes, the talent show." Ben cups his chin in his hand. "Remind me again, who in this family has won the talent show three years in a row?"

I roll my eyes as hard as I can. Ben's in high school now and has been taking piano lessons since he was six. As much as I hate to admit it, he is very good. I, on the other

3

Take a Breath Olive Tran

hand, took lessons for two months before my mom decided it was best for everyone involved that I try something else. Ditto for violin. And guitar. And...grimace... drums.

"I dunno, it must have been Mom." I stick out my tongue at him. "We all know you're some sort of piano prodigy, Ben. How could we possibly forget when you keep reminding us?"

Ben smirks at me. He seems to have some friends, so I assume that he's only this obnoxious at home. To be fair, though, not only did he win three years in a row, but because of him, the school made a rule that winners can't enter the contest the next year after their win. It's a wonder he's even able to lift that big head of his.

Phuong Truong

He sneaks a look at my notebook and raises his eyebrows. It's covered in doodles and scribbles and a drawing of a pony that looks suspiciously like a tall cow. There's not one single idea listed. "You know, the talent show is optional. You don't have to enter if you don't have any talents."

I shut the notebook with a snap. "Not only am I going to enter, but I'm going to win!"

Ben just shrugs.

I have talents. I have *lots* of talents. I just don't know what they are yet.

Chapter 2

We all breathe a sigh of relief after finishing a not-particularly-interesting lesson on pulleys and gears. Mr. Chu is a great teacher, but even he can't make the inside workings of a clock fun. At least he's given up trying to copy the chimney sweep's Cockney accent from *Mary Poppins*. He kept it up for most of the morning after we watched the movie in class, but no one could understand what he was saying.

Phuong Truong

"Kids, I have a small announcement to make before you go for your lunch," calls out Mr. Chu after he's put away his bin of science supplies. "As you probably know, the Maple Avenue Elementary Mid-Year Talent Show is happening in a little more than three weeks."

There's a rustle of excitement as my classmates perk up, once again alert. "As usual, the winner of the show gets a pizza party for their class. Sadly, teachers cannot participate, so you guys are on your own." Hands shoot into the air. "Yes, Simon?"

"Can anyone enter the contest?"

"Any student or group of students, grades four and up, may enter." This is the first year that the kids in my class can enter, so there's lots of excited chattering. Mr. Chu lifts his

Take a Breath Olive Tran

hands to the class as if to hold back the tide of over-enthusiastic performers. "I do encourage you to put some thought into your act. While *I* may think it's really cool that you can touch your nose with your tongue or cross your eyes on command, it may be difficult to use these abilities to entertain a crowd for more than a few seconds." A bunch of kids lower their hands.

"That said, I will repeat, anyone can enter the competition. And while I can't enter the contest myself, I would be more than happy to lend you some of my expert advice." Mr. Chu winks and tips an invisible hat. "Emily, you have a question?"

"What kind of acts are most likely to win?" Emily is the sportiest kid in our class. She always wins all the sprints, even beating

Take a Breath Olive Tran

out the boys, and almost never misses a shot when she's on the basketball court. I think she's just started archery lessons. Ohhh, maybe she could shoot an arrow at some targets. She could hit an apple sitting on someone's head! That would be so cool.

"Good question, Emily. I find that everyone loves a good laugh, so something fun. Or maybe a dramatic monologue from your favorite movie? Or the latest dances? The floss...the dab...the sprinkler?!" Mr. Chu demonstrates each move and definitely loses all expert credibility. Some kids groan, some giggle, but we're all relieved when the lunch bell rings and puts a stop to Mr. Chu's show. "Oof, I've worked up a bit of a sweat. All right, lunchtime everyone!"

Chapter 3

As soon as Penny, Ella, Mia, and I sit down at our usual table at the far side of the lunchroom, I get down to business. "So, girls, what are we gonna do?"

"About what?" asks Ella before taking a bite of her pasta salad.

"The talent show, of course!" We were just talking about it five minutes ago, how could she have already put it out of her mind? "Don't you want to win? We *have* to get that pizza party."

11

Take a Breath Olive Tran

"Oh...I'm not entering. There's no way I'm getting up on stage and have everyone looking at me, especially if I don't even get marks for it." Ella gives a little shudder. "Ugh, not for all of the ice cream sundaes in the world."

Hmmm, Ella is an ice cream fanatic, so she must be serious. Her backpack has a pattern of little ice cream cones all over it, her bedroom could pass for an ice cream parlor (though her parents did draw the line at a personal freezer), and—no surprise—she has an ice cream cake for her birthday every year. There's a small town in Iowa that calls itself the ice cream capital of the world, and Mr. and Mrs. Cohen said they would take her for her thirteenth birthday. I'm not sure what else there is to do there, so they're probably hoping this is just a phase she grows out of by then.

"Who won last year?" asks Mia. Her dad has packed her a cucumber and cream cheese sandwich today, no crusts. Mr. Ahmad also puts a little note or drawing in her lunch bag every day. Mia smiles to herself as she tucks today's note away. So cute! "Maybe that'll give us some ideas?"

"Liam Henry won last year," I answer. "Remember? He brought his dog and they did all these tricks together." Good thing he can't enter again this year 'cause they were pretty awesome. "Does anyone have any talented pets?" I look around hopefully.

"Bert and Ernie follow my finger when I trace patterns on the outside of their tank..." says Ella. Bert and Ernie are her goldfish.

Take a Breath Olive Tran

I don't have any fish, but I kinda think they all do that.

"It may be hard to make that into an entire act," I say doubtfully. Ella looks relieved that I've let her off the hook (pun intended), but I appreciate that she volunteered her fish.

"Sorry, but my bunny, Mr. Floof, doesn't really do a whole lot," adds Mia. "He hops and eats. And poops. He hops and eats and poops. That's all."

"Okay, no pet tricks." This is going to be a little harder than I thought. "Any other ideas?"

"How about music?" suggests Penny. She's got a hamburger for lunch, but all she's done so far is make a little pile of the sesame seeds she's picked off the bun. Funny, I

14

Take a Breath Olive Tran

don't remember her ever having a problem with sesame seeds. "We could do a song?"

"Ugh, I wish," I groan. "I can't carry a tune at all. And I have no sense of rhythm. Even shaking a tambourine is hard!"

"Does this mean you won't be doing the floss on stage?" giggles Mia.

"One hundred percent." It's my turn to shudder.

Chapter 4

"Mom! I'm home!" I drop my backpack by the door and kick off my shoes. I slide my house slippers on and head to the kitchen for my after-school snack.

"Hi, sweetie," she calls out from her studio. "I'm just finishing up this last bit. Be out in a minute!" Mom is an artist. She works with all kinds of stuff—paint, yarn, and most recently, clay. But just like with Ben, none of her abilities have rubbed off on me. I guess I'm just not destined for a life in the arts.

Take a Breath Olive Tran

"Hi, Bà Nội." Bà Nội is putting groceries away, so I help unpack the bags. This scores me points for being helpful and also gives me a chance to scope out what goodies we have before Ben gets to them.

"Hi, Con. You want grill cheese?"

"Ooh, yes please." My grandma doesn't usually make non-Vietnamese food, but she does make an amazing grilled cheese sandwich. She always makes sure to spread the butter right to the edges of the bread so that every bite is crispy and delicious.

"Okay, you put food away. I cook." She gets the cheese from the fridge—sharp cheddar for taste, mozzarella for the pull—and cuts some slices off the loaf of sourdough bread. "I make one for you mom too. She not eat enough."

18

Take a Breath Olive Tran

The groceries are taken care of and the sandwiches are sizzling in the pan when Mom finds her way to the kitchen. "Mmm, that smells good."

"Bà Nội's making grilled cheese sandwiches, and she's making one for you too!" I say as Mom pulls up a seat at the counter.

"Thanks, Má."

The sandwiches are placed in front of us, but before Mom can take a bite, I blurt out, "Can we get a dog?" I've been burning to ask her since lunch.

"What? Why?" Mom gives me a funny look. "No, but still why?" Then she takes a bite and shuts her eyes, sighing. "You've never asked for a pet before, and correct me if I'm wrong, but aren't you scared of dogs?"

Phuong Truong

"Maybe I've grown out of that?" I suggest hopefully. But who am I kidding? One of my earliest memories is being chased by a neighbor's cockapoo. It was terrifying. Buttons doesn't seem nearly as big to me as she did when I was three years old, but I still flinch whenever she comes to say hello. "The talent show is in three weeks, and I need to come up with an idea. Last year, Liam did tricks with his dog and won, so I thought I could do the same thing."

"Olive!" Mom laughs. "It takes a long time to train a dog. You couldn't possibly have an act ready in three weeks. Besides, don't you want to do something more original?"

"I would do something original if I could think of something," I moan. "I think I was passed over when all the artistic talents

21

were handed out to this family. Or maybe you and Ben are so good at stuff that you sucked up more than your fair share of artsy-ness. You two are artsy-ness hoggers!"

"Eh, don't forget Bà Nội sing real good," chimes in Grandma. Bà Nội has been known to perform some cải lương songs at the community center on Vietnamese karaoke night. It's a type of Vietnamese opera or folk music. I find it kinda screechy, which I would never admit to her in a million years, but her friends seem to enjoy her singing.

Mom tries—and fails—to smother her laughter. "Olive, you're good at lots of things. I can't think of what you might be able to do in front of an audience, but I'm sure you'll think of something."

Phuong Truong

"Well, putting groceries away is not going to win me any prizes," I mumble. "Hey, where's Ben? Maybe he can give me some ideas."

"He said he had something to do after school today so he'll be a little late."

Blurgh. Nothing is going my way today. It looks like, as usual, I'll only be able to count on one person to come up with an idea. Me.

Chapter 5

I look for inspiration where all the ideas live: the internet. I park myself in the den in front of the computer Ben and I share and type in, "Best talent show ideas." The search brings up a long list of possible acts, lots of which I've already nixed (basically anything related to music or dance or theater). The first quirky suggestion is ventriloquism. Click.

Ventriloquism is an act that involves speaking without really moving your lips,

24

Phuong Truong

so it appears like the speaker's voice is coming from somewhere else, often a puppet or dummy. Also known as "throwing your voice."

I look at my left hand, now formed into a puppet shape. Well, I guess it's more of a big beak. I can do this! Can I do this? "Hello, my name is Fingers McGee," I say out of the corner of my mouth. I think I'm a natural.

Ohhh, there are videos. It couldn't hurt to watch one. Maybe three or four, just so I can figure out some details.

☆

I may have watched a few more videos than I had set out to. There are, surprisingly, lots

25

Take a Breath Olive Tran

of ventriloquists out there. The dummies can take any form, from dolls to animals to even skeletons and aliens! Most of the acts are funny and the ventriloquists tell jokes. But some of them do other things, like sing—how can people sing without moving their mouths?!—or dance. I even saw a dummy hypnotize its ventriloquist!

I'll have to start simple. Jokes should be easy enough. Knock-knock jokes would get the audience to participate. I've barely started and I can already feel my show coming together. People will be crying from laughing so hard. My class is gonna love me for winning them the pizza party!

Okay, let's do this. I raise my left hand and bring Fingers McGee back to life. *"Hello...."*

26

Take a Breath Olive Tran

"Why are you talking to your hand?" Ben asks. Gah, where did he come from?

"I'm not talking to my hand," I respond. "I'm talking to my buddy."

Ben's expression goes from confused to possibly worried. "Your buddy?"

I turn Fingers McGee to face my brother. *"Hello! I'm Fingers McGee!"*

Ben is back to looking confused.

"It's my act for the talent show! I'm going to do ventriloquism."

"But I can see your lips moving," says Ben. "Isn't that the whole point of ventriloquism? To make it look like the dummy is talking?"

"My lips aren't moving," I protest. I try again. *"Hello! I'm Fingers McGee and I'm totally talking all by myself!"*

28

Phuong Truong

"Olive, your lips are clearly moving. And not just a little," Ben scoffs. "Anyway, Mom said to get you for dinner. I'm hungry, so make it snappy."

Wahhhhhh. I was so sure that I'd done it, that I'd cracked the talent show code. Victory was mine!

On the bright side, Bà Nội is in charge of dinner tonight. Mom is a good cook too, but she mostly makes stuff like meat loaf and spaghetti. Bà Nội almost always makes Vietnamese food, which is my comfort food. I could use a little something to re-group and come up with a new plan. And nothing is as comforting as a big, steaming bowl of phở.

Chapter 6

I wake up the next morning feeling like I haven't slept a wink. Sleeping is my favorite activity and, usually, my superpower. I was sure that as soon as I snuggled into bed with Wishful Thinking Pony safe in the crook of my arm, my mind would clear and ideas for the talent show would flood my brain.

But I couldn't relax. I couldn't get comfortable. I tossed and turned and tried out different sleeping positions, but nothing

30

Take a Breath Olive Tran

worked. I definitely couldn't clear my thoughts. Every time I closed my eyes, it felt like the walls were closing in on me. And the dummies! Dummies of every shape and size, singing, and dancing, and laughing. Laughing *at* me, not with me.

It was awful.

I never believed it before, but maybe there *is* such a thing as too much screen time?

I make it to school, but everything seems too bright and too loud. I sit at my desk, head resting on one hand, my other hand picking idly at some crud on my jeans that I'd thought were clean. Then Mr. Chu says possibly the worst thing ever.

"Good morning! Everyone, please clear your desks for your science test!"

Phuong Truong

Oh noooooooo. I had completely forgotten that we were being tested on the Pulleys and Gears unit. While I low-key love quizzes and tests of every kind—there's nothing quite like the rush of getting a perfect score—today I am not ready. I didn't do any review last night and everything's feeling a little fuzzy.

I glance down at the test and sigh in relief. It's multiple choice! There's still a chance I can do well on this.

First question: What must you have to set something in motion?

A: a pulley

B: a gear

C: force

D: a plan

Take a Breath Olive Tran

They all kinda sound like good answers, so I know I'm in trouble. I take a deep breath, circle a random response, and hope for the best.

Chapter 7

What a week! I managed to eke out a decent mark on my science test (73%—not up to my usual standards, but good enough not to catch any attention), and I had to work extra hard to stay on top of all my homework. It's been so tough to focus on schoolwork with the talent show looming over me. And since it's taken so long to do my work, I haven't had enough time to brainstorm ideas.

Worst of all, I still have not been sleeping well. You would think that with all that

Take a Breath Olive Tran

extra awake time, I could come up with something great, but nothing seems good enough. I had considered just signing up anyway, but the thought of having to pull out of the show in disgrace was too much to bear.

I *have* ruled out lots though. Juggling: I don't have the hand-eye coordination to keep two items in the air, let alone three or four. Luckily, Mom stopped me from using the eggs I'd pulled out of the fridge to practice with and gave me some old tennis balls from the garage. That would have been a mess!

Comedy: it turns out that while I'm plenty funny, it's not actually that easy to come up with even five minutes of material and keep an audience laughing. Even my favorite knock-knock joke fell flat.

—Knock, knock!

—Who's there?

—Howl.

—Howl who?

—Howl you know if you don't open the door?!

Classic! I tested out my set on Bà Nội, and all I got was crickets. Not literally, but the silence was deafening. Maybe the jokes were lost in translation? In any case, I decided to move on.

There were other ideas, like jumping rope or Hula-Hooping. While I can do them just fine, I fail to see how they can be entertaining. Maybe if I added fire or something, but I'm pretty sure that would break six or seven school rules.

Big giant sigh.

Phuong Truong

I flop over to lie on my back in the grass. It's afternoon recess and Penny brought her Uno cards. "What's wrong, Olive?" she asks as she puts down a red two. "You've been so quiet lately, and you've barely even touched your lunch. I know how much you love your granny's bánh mì!"

I use my arm to block the sun from my upturned face. "Ugh, I'm just tired. I haven't been able to sleep. And I still haven't come up with an idea for the talent show and sign up ends today!"

"Why do you wanna do it so badly?" Ella puts down another two, this time green. She only has one card left in her hand. "Uno."

I uncover my eyes to stare at her. "Don't you want to win the pizza party? It would be so much fun!"

Take a Breath Olive Tran

"Sure," she shrugs, "but it's just pizza."

I sit up straight. "It's not just pizza! It's the *experience*. It's time out of our school day to have fun. It's something we'll remember for the rest of our lives!"

Mia side-eyes me as she picks up a card and ends her turn. "Is it also about the attention? Why do *you* have to win the party, Olive?"

"Well, it doesn't have to be me, but I really want this party for *usss*. I can't just sit around doing nothing." I tap my chin with my finger. "Matt is doing tricks with his guinea pig. Everyone loves animals, but a guinea pig is no puppy."

"I think Emily is juggling?" adds Ella. I'm kinda impressed since I couldn't juggle at all, but I'm still doubtful of the entertainment value.

40

Phuong Truong

I scoff, and Penny shoots a quick frown at me. I sheepishly place a green eight on the pile.

"Oh, and Josh is doing magic tricks," says Mia. Hmmm, that sounds more promising.

"Don't you think you're being a little hard on everyone, Olive?" asks Penny with a bite in her voice that I don't think I've heard before. "I think anyone who has the guts to get on stage in front of the whole school deserves a little credit."

"That's for sure," says Ella. She grimaces at even the thought of being in the spotlight.

I sit up. "But don't you want us to win?" I ask Penny.

"Winning isn't everything, Olive." Penny's cheeks are bright red, which I know means she's very upset. I just don't get why.

41

Take a Breath Olive Tran

"Kids are going to be standing under all those bright lights, trying their best to put on a show for everyone. They don't need people like *you* judging them and making snarky comments about their performance!"

Penny slams down her last three cards, all eights. "I win." Then she gets up and stomps back toward the school.

Ella, Mia, and I are all a little stunned. The bell rings, and we gather up her cards and silently trudge back to class.

42

Chapter 8

It's officially over. I missed the deadline to sign up for the talent show. Every second that ticked away on the clock over our classroom door seemed to echo in my head, mocking me for being unable come up with an idea. I couldn't even think straight. The blowup with Penny just made everything feel a million times worse.

They say victory is sweet, but I guess I won't ever find out. Failure doesn't taste like anything. It feels like dark clouds. Like

Phuong Truong

emptiness. On second thought, failure does taste like something. It tastes like mushy, overcooked, boiled brussels sprouts. It tastes like sadness.

The short walk from school seems to take forever. Each step is an effort. I finally make it home and drag myself up the few steps to our front door. Inside, I manage to slide my bag off my back, but taking my shoes off is too much. I lie down in the hallway, my feet still resting in the designated outdoor shoe area by the door. I may be upset, but I still remember how much Bà Nội hates having shoes inside. A scolding is the last thing I need.

"Olive? Is that you?" my mom calls out from her studio.

"Mrmph."

45

Take a Breath Olive Tran

She comes to investigate and finds me lying on the floor. "Oh dear. Bad day?"

"The worst. I couldn't come up with an act for the talent show and I've missed the sign-up deadline," I whisper. "And Penny is mad at me, and I don't even really know why. Is the room spinning? It feels like the room is spinning."

"Hang on," says Mom. She goes into the kitchen, and I hear her rifling through a cupboard. When she comes back, she crouches down by my head. "Take a few deep breaths." My first attempt sounds more like a hiccup, but by the fourth long exhale, I'm starting to feel more steady. "Now, open up."

I open my mouth. Mom places a small piece of emergency chocolate in my mouth.

46

Phuong Truong

Milk chocolate, not dark, 'cause yuck. Emergency chocolate is supposed to make you feel better, not worse. It's something my mom has done ever since Ben and I were little. If we were ever sad or hurt, she would slip us a bit of chocolate. By the time the chocolate melted on our tongues (no chewing allowed), we'd be calmer.

Just like now. "Better?" she asks.

Sigh. "A little. There's only one of you now."

Mom takes off my shoes and helps me up, and then she makes me a cup of tea. She must feel really bad for me, 'cause she lets me put as much milk and sugar in it as I want, which is a lot. She often says that if I stuck a spoon in my cup of tea, it would stick straight up.

47

Take a Breath Olive Tran

"Do you want to talk about it?" Mom takes a sip of her own boring, bland tea. No sugar in it at all.

"Not really," I say, cradling the hot cup in my hands. "Maybe. I guess I just feel like I've let everyone down."

My mom looks confused. "How does you not entering the talent contest let everyone down?"

"I wanted my class to get the pizza party. But I can't win it for us now. It's all out of my hands." My plans for an epic year are ruined.

"Oh, Olive." Mom rubs soothing circles on my back. "I don't think anyone expected you to win the party for them. Is it possible that you're putting all of this pressure on yourself?"

48

"But Ben won the talent show three years in a row!" I point out. "Everyone's expecting me to carry on the family tradition!"

"Olive, I'm sure you'll agree that you and Ben are completely different people." I nod slowly. "You have different interests and different strengths. Just because he did the talent show doesn't mean that you have to. And one person hardly makes a tradition."

"I suppose," I mumble. "But I want you to be proud of me, too. And I really wanted to wiiiiin."

"I am proud of you! I'm proud of the person you are. Your humor, and your intelligence, and, most of all, your kindness. Winning an elementary school talent show really doesn't have much to

Take a Breath Olive Tran

do with anything. Besides, winning isn't everything." I roll my eyes at this. "I know, I know. It sounds very corny, but it's true. If you really want your class to win this party, maybe there's some other way you could be involved? Or maybe it's enough for you to cheer them on?"

I just shrug. That doesn't seem at all exciting, kind of a letdown, really.

"And what's happening between you and Penny?" she asks.

"I don't really know." I stir my tea a lot harder than it probably needs. "We were playing Uno, and I was talking about being stressed at not having a talent show idea... and she just exploded!"

Mom frowns. "That doesn't sound very much like Penny at all," she says. "Maybe it

50

Phuong Truong

was just a misunderstanding and it'll blow over soon? Talk to her tomorrow." She rubs my back some more. "Now, would it be mean of me to ask you to tell me something that you've learned today?" This is a game Mom and I play, a question that she's asked me almost every single day for as long as I can remember.

"I learned that winning isn't everything?" I reply flatly.

"Ha, smarty pants," Mom chuckles. "I will accept that response today and hope that someday you will actually believe it."

I just shrug again.

"I know what might cheer you up. Ben should be home in a couple of hours. I have to finish up a project, but why don't the two of you go see a movie tonight? On me, snacks included."

Take a Breath Olive Tran

I perk up at the idea of a night at the movies. For the first time in a long time, I have something to look forward to.

Chapter 9

"What? Why do I have to take you to the movies?" Ben has just gotten home from whatever after-school activity and dropped his bag on the kitchen floor.

"Because I'm asking you to," Mom tells him. "Your sister is feeling down, so you're gonna help cheer her up. I would take her, but I need to finish up some work tonight." Ben gives her a dark look and she quickly adds, "I'll pay for everything. And I'll drop you off and pick you up afterward."

Take a Breath Olive Tran

His face clears. "Okay, fine. Does this count as your birthday gift?"

"No way!" I'm quick to shoot that down. "Mom's paying for everything, so it's basically a gift from her." For my birthday, Ben had given me a coupon he'd made for dinner and a movie with him. I love movies, and I love food even more, so it was a surprisingly thoughtful gift. I got some pretty cool presents—books, candy, stuffies—but his gift was probably my favorite.

"Fiiiiine," Ben says, rolling his eyes. "Though it should totally count. Can we go now? I'm starving."

☆

"Ugh, this sucks." Ben doesn't seem too impressed by the movie selection. Our nearby movie theater has four screens. Tonight they're showing *Love and Coffee* (a romantic comedy about a barista who mixes up special drinks and makes love matches for all her customers—so cheesy); *Die Eiche* (a drama from Germany about death—err, snoozefest); *Fightmare V: Never Wake Up* (a horror movie that thankfully we're both too young to get into); and...wait for it...*Magic Sparkle Fairy Ponies: Journey to Putopia* (only the best movie ever, no description necessary).

"Haven't you already seen that pony movie?" he whines. "I'd rather get some food and stare at a wall for two hours."

Take a Breath Olive Tran

"Now, Ben," I remind him, "how would Mom feel if she found out you left your little sister in the movie theater all by herself? And yes, I've already seen it, but I want to watch it again." Penny, Ella, Mia, and I had seen it on opening weekend and it was *amazing*. If I could, I'd watch it every day! "Let's get some food. You're just hangry. Besides, I think you're going to like it."

"I doubt that a hot dog is really going to change my mind," he mutters, and we head inside to get our tickets.

Ben opts for a slice of pepperoni pizza and I go for the nachos. Boy, he must have been really hungry, 'cause he scarfs down his food and thinks about going back for more. I have about half of my nachos left, so I slide them over. I've gotta save room

56

Phuong Truong

for popcorn, anyway. We finish up, get our snacks, and find our seats with ten minutes left until show time.

"So, what's got you so down, anyway?" Ben takes a sip of his soda and helps himself to some of my popcorn.

"Ugh, it's the stupid talent show," I say between my own mouthfuls of popcorn. I have to make sure I get some before he eats it all! "I couldn't come up with an act, and the sign-up deadline was today, so I guess I'm not going to be in it."

"That again? What's the big deal?" Thankfully, he's switched to eating the chocolate-covered peanuts he chose for himself. At least he didn't get raisins this time. Raisins are gross and no one will ever be able to convince me otherwise.

57

Take a Breath Olive Tran

"You're the one who keeps reminding me you've won it three times!" I sputter. I grab a handful of his chocolates, 'cause fair is fair. "I just...you made it seem so easy. I wanted to win so badly, and my class would get a party, and everyone would be happy and love me."

"So, you wanted to be the hero?" He raises his eyebrows.

I think about it. Was this why I had lost so much sleep and most of my appetite over the last week? "Yeah, I guess. Doesn't everyone?"

"Maybe...maybe not? It seems like you're putting a lot of unnecessary pressure on yourself. Maybe you shouldn't try to force it? Let someone else be the hero. You may be surprised at who steps up to the plate."

Phuong Truong

If I could use an emoji to describe my face, it would be "expressionless." I have no confidence in Ben's advice. "Aaaand, I don't even know how it happened, but Penny's mad at me."

Ben shrugs. "You never know what people have going on in their lives. Maybe you should cut her some slack, too. Stop going all 'Olive' on her."

The lights dim, so I can't tell if he sees the offended look I shoot him, and the music starts. Ben starts tapping his fingers along to the theme song, perfectly in time. He must be flexing those piano prodigy muscles again. Almost immediately, I get swept away in the world of *Magic Sparkle Fairy Ponies*, where happy endings are always guaranteed.

59

Take a Breath Olive Tran

☆

After a glorious hour and a half, the lights come back on. I look over at Ben, who is trying to quietly blow his nose. His eyes look kinda wet, too.

"Ben! Are you crying?!" I laugh.

"Those ponies...they're always there for each other." He takes a shuddering breath. "You're right, this was a great movie."

I consider the kids in my class who have signed up for the show. Ben and the ponies could be onto something. Every pony had a different magic and they had to work together to obtain the crystal that would stop the never-ending winter. Teamwork makes the dream work, so if we want that pizza party, we might just have to do the same.

60

Chapter 10

I finally got a good night's sleep. I guess I was finally able to relax once I accepted I wouldn't be performing. I realized that I didn't need to be in the spotlight, or be the hero, like Ben suggested. I just don't like to feel helpless. I need to feel like I've shaped my own destiny.

Which is why I'm on my way to Josh's house on a Saturday morning. I've asked Emily and Matt to meet us here, so I get myself in the right frame of mind by

Take a Breath Olive Tran

repeating some mantras that I found—where else?—on the internet. *Teamwork makes the dream work. There's no "I" in team. Together we can accomplish great things.*

Josh lives just down the street from me and we've known each other since forever. He is for sure my best boy friend...friend that is a boy.

He's waiting outside on his front step when I arrive, a deck of cards in his hands. "Hi, Olive!"

"Hey, Josh!" I sit beside him on the step. "Thanks for letting us meet here."

"Oh, I didn't think I had a choice," he laughs, shuffling the cards. "Your requests can sound pretty commanding sometimes.

62

You can be downright scary, Olive."

"Huh, I disagree," I say. "I'm always perfectly pleasant. There's nothing wrong with being confident and assertive."

"Sure." Josh gives me a pretty impressive side-eye. He's also smiling, so I don't take it personally. "So, what's up? What scheme do you have planned?"

"Scheme? Why does there have to be a scheme? I'm *wounded*," I proclaim.

"Well, let's see. You don't really spend much time with Emily and Matt outside of school, you've never asked them to come to my house, and you kinda always have some wild idea cooking," he points out.

"Okay, so maybe I do have an idea about the talent show." I sneak a peek at Josh,

Phuong Truong

who seems unfazed. It's kind of nice to have friends who know you so well. "I'll explain when the others get here."

We don't have to wait very long. Not a minute later, Emily arrives, and Matt rolls up not long after that. We stand up to greet them.

"Hey, guys," says Matt. "So, Olive, what are you scheming? I assume this meeting was your idea?"

Josh grins and shoots me a look, which I ignore.

"Hi Matt, Emily. Glad you both could make it, and yes, this was my idea." I take a deep breath. "It's about the talent show."

Emily tilts her head and Matt raises his eyebrows. At least I know I've piqued their interest!

65

Take a Breath Olive Tran

"I'm sure we would all agree that it would be amazing if someone in our class won the talent show, so we could have a pizza party, which we will remember for the rest of our lives."

I didn't think it was possible, but Matt's eyebrows go even higher. "We're talking about a pizza party, right?"

"Yeah, Olive," adds Emily, "doesn't just about everyone have a pizza party for their birthday?"

Oh no. I'm losing them! Why am I the only one who can see the bigger picture? I need to get this meeting back on track. "Yes, but are they during school? During what would normally be a boring math or history lesson?"

Phuong Truong

"I like those subjects..." mutters Josh, and I elbow him.

I forge ahead. "I was hoping to be in the talent show myself, but couldn't come up with anything to perform. Then, as I was watching the *Magic Sparkle Fairy Ponies* movie again—"

"Ohmygod! Wasn't that movie just the best!" exclaims Emily. Matt and Josh roll their eyes.

"Yes! It is definitely the best," I agree. "And, most importantly, it reminded me that you can do anything if you work as a team."

"I still don't get it," says Matt. "What does your stupid pony movie have to do with the talent show?" This earns him a glare from Emily.

Take a Breath Olive Tran

"While I think that your acts are great," I pause to look at each of them, "I think that if we combine them all into one megashow, they would be fantastic!"

"Err, Olive? How do we combine Emily's juggling, Matt's guinea pig—"

"Mr. Beast!" insists Matt.

Josh nods. "How do we combine Emily's juggling, Mr. Beast, and my magic tricks?" Josh asks.

"With a little creativity and a lot of teamwork!" I answer with flair, my arms shooting into the air like I've just finished a gymnastics routine.

My flourish doesn't seem to convince them entirely, but they agree to give it a try. They each describe what they're planning

Phuong Truong

to do, and I promise to think about how to meld the three acts into one. I've assured them that if I can't come up with a way to do it, they're free to continue their solo acts.

Chapter 11

I did it!

Well, I *think* I did it, and I managed to convince Josh, Emily, and Matt that combining their acts was a solid plan, so for everyone's sake (but mostly mine), I hope this works out. We've met at lunch every day for the last two weeks, and I may not be completely objective, but I think we have a real shot at taking home the big prize. I mean they. *They* have a great shot.

Phuong Truong

And today is the big day. The Maple Avenue Elementary School Mid-Year Talent Show.

After gobbling down a quick dinner of takeout sushi rolls and miso soup, Mom, Bà Nội, and I head back to school for the show. We've all gone to enough school events to know that if we don't get there early, all the good seats will be gone. Ben's not home—I guess he's busy doing whatever he's been up to after school for the last few weeks—and won't be joining us.

My family takes their seats (third row, center stage!), while I go backstage to look for my team. I find them huddled around Mr. Beast's cage. "Hi guys! Is everyone ready?"

"I think Mr. Beast might be a little nervous," says Matt.

Take a Breath Olive Tran

Mr. Beast is eating a carrot and looks pretty much the same as he always does. I raise my eyebrows and look at Josh, who just shrugs. I think Matt may be projecting his own feelings onto his pet.

"Well, Mr. Beast, I think you're going to do great!" I give the cage a small pat, which Mr. Beast ignores. "You guys are all going to do great." I look them each in the eyes, 'cause that's what good coaches do. "Emily, how are you feeling?"

Emily is rotating her wrists back and forth, while also doing some lunges to keep her muscles warm. "I'm okay. Just doing some stretches."

"Good, good. All good." In the movies, this is when the coach gives the team an inspiring pep talk that carries them to victory. I don't

72

Phuong Truong

know if I have that in me, but I give it a shot. "So, this is the day we've all been working towards. I know there was some doubt in the beginning, but I think that we've really banded together and formed a strong team with strong bonds. And if you perform just as well tonight as you have in your last few practices, you're going to be hard to beat. But no matter what happens out there, just have fun and know that I'm proud of you."

"Thanks, Mom," laughs Josh.

I shoot him some stink-eye for ruining my dramatic moment. "Okay, fine. Break a leg, everyone!" I give Emily a quick hug and fist-bump each of the boys.

Back in my seat, I'm happy to find that Mia and her dad are sitting next to us. The show is about to begin, so I give them

73

a quick greeting and settle in for the first performance.

☆

There are only two acts left to go, and my team is up next. So far, we've seen multiple dance troupes, a stand-up comedian, a puppet show, and two kids playing the recorder. Some acts are better than others—you'll never be able to convince me that anything played on a recorder sounds good—and our chances are looking good.

The curtain opens and Josh walks on stage wearing a black cape and a large top hat. "Good evening, ladies and gentlemen! I am Josh the Great and tonight I will be performing some feats of magic! Trust me

Phuong Truong

when I say that you won't believe your eyes! But first, let me introduce my assistant, Emily!"

Emily enters the stage and waves to the audience. Since I couldn't convince her to wear a special sparkly outfit, she's wearing the same clothes she had on in class today: jeans and a purple sweatshirt. "We're going to start off with a card trick," announces Josh. "Emily, please shuffle this deck of cards well." Josh hands her the deck and she does as instructed. "Now, please select a card from the deck, any card you like. Show it to the audience, but make sure that I can't see it." He makes a big show of turning away from Emily and her card.

Emily picks a card and holds it up to the audience. An eight of diamonds.

Take a Breath Olive Tran

"Please place your card back in the deck and shuffle it again." Josh places the newly shuffled deck in his left hand and circles his right hand over the deck. "I'm getting a reading from these cards...give me a minute...." He pulls a card from the deck and shows it to the crowd. "Is it the king of hearts?"

The audience calls out, "Nooooo!"

Josh looks worried and pulls another card from the deck. "The four of spades?!"

"Nooooo!" the audience says again.

He hurriedly selects another card. "The five of diamonds?!"

"Noooo!" they say again. Someone feels badly for Josh and adds, "Close, though!"

"Well, there must be something wrong with these cards. Assistant Emily, please

Phuong Truong

remove these from my sight!" Emily takes the cards and places them on the floor.

The audience starts to fidget, nervous for Josh the Great. "For my next trick, I'll pull a rabbit from my hat!" He walks to the table on the stage and takes the top hat from his head, placing it upside down on the table. Josh reaches down into the hat, making sure to rummage about, and pulls out a plastic apple. "Hmm, this is not a rabbit!" He tosses the apple behind him to a waiting Emily.

Again, he feels around in his hat, this time pulling out an orange. "This is also not a rabbit!" The plastic orange goes over his shoulder, again to Emily. This time, she looks at the two fruits in her hands, shrugs, and starts to juggle them. Josh pulls out

Take a Breath Olive Tran

another item from his hat: a pear. "Where is that rabbit?!" He throws the pear over his shoulder to Emily, who smoothly adds it to the fruit she's juggling between her hands. The crowd starts to cheer.

"But I haven't found the rabbit!" exclaims Josh to the crowd. "One last try." He makes a big show of feeling every inch inside the hat. "Aha!" He pulls out a guinea pig.

"Oh, this is still not a rabbit!" he says and goes to toss the guinea pig behind him. Emily squeaks and drops the plastic fruit she's been juggling, readying to catch the guinea pig. The audience gasps. "But you're close enough," continues Josh, placing the guinea pig gently on the table. The audience laughs and cheers.

Phuong Truong

From offstage, Matt calls out, "Mr. Beast! You found him!" He comes out to collect his pet. "I've been looking for him everywhere. Thank you, Josh the Great!"

Before Matt can pick up Mr. Beast, he scampers off the table. Mr. Beast leads the kids on a merry chase all over the stage, managing to knock over the deck of cards that had been set down earlier. Matt finally scoops him up. "Got you!"

Josh stops Matt before he can exit the stage. "What's that Mr. Beast has in his mouth?"

"Oh, sorry," says Matt. "He's got one of your cards." Matt takes the card from Mr. Beast and hands it to Josh.

"Ladies and gentlemen, let's have a look at the card Mr. Beast has selected." He holds it up to the audience. "The eight of diamonds!" The crowd roars, and Josh, Emily, and Matt take their bows. Matt holds Mr. Beast with two hands and lifts him high to receive his glory, and they all quickly run offstage.

It went amazing. As well as I could have dreamed. I'm still riding the emotional high when the last act is announced.

"Wow, what a great performance by the Chu Chums!" says our principal, Ms. Gomez. "Now, our last performer is also from Mr. Chu's grade four class. With a special appearance by Maple Avenue Talent Show hall-of-famer, Ben Tran, here is Penny Harris!"

Chapter 12

Ben? Penny?! What is happening?

The curtains pull back to reveal Ben sitting at a piano off to the side and Penny standing front and center behind a microphone. She's wearing a beautiful, sparkling white dress and matching headband. Ugh, I knew sparkles would look amazing under all the lights! For a split second, I imagine myself onstage, but my envy is soon smothered by a pang of hurt. Why didn't she tell me about this? Why didn't he?

Phuong Truong

Penny looks back and gives Ben a tiny nod. He starts to play a gentle, lilting melody.

OMG, I would recognize that music anywhere! It's the *Magic Sparkle Fairy Ponies* theme song! Penny starts to sing, and all thoughts empty out of my head.

"...Friendship lasts foreveeeeer!"

Penny is magical. More magical than even Wishful Thinking Pony, my favorite of the Magic Sparkle Fairy Ponies. The audience, silent and rapt just a second ago, stands and cheers. Mia and I, probably the loudest in the room, wipe tears from our eyes and clutch each other as we jump up and down.

Penny and Ben take their bows and rush backstage.

Take a Breath Olive Tran

Minutes later, all of the contestants are brought back out for the results. The school's method for determining the winner is simple: the act that gets the most overall applause wins. The audience can clap for as many acts as they like, so everyone gets some applause from friends and family, but the loudest cheers are usually reserved for the best.

As expected, everyone gets a moderate amount of applause. The Chu Chums do fairly well and get a better response than any of the previous acts. But it's no surprise when it feels like the roof is going to get blown off as Penny's name is called. She looks genuinely surprised and thrilled when she shakes Ms. Gomez's hand and accepts her trophy.

Phuong Truong

"Congratulations, Penny Harris! In addition to this lovely trophy you've received tonight, you have won a pizza party for your entire class! Well done!"

Penny holds up her trophy, and the cheering reaches a new high. My class is getting the pizza party, something I've wanted to make happen so badly these last few weeks, and at this moment, I couldn't care less.

Chapter 13

Mom, Bà Nội, and I wait outside the school with Penny's parents.

"Peter, Neil, you must be so proud of Penny! She sang so beautifully!" says Mom.

"We definitely are," says Neil. "And thanks so much for letting us borrow Ben these last few weeks. He really helped Penny with her nerves."

When Ben finally appears, he gets a hug from Mom and a "Very good" from Bà Nội. I punch him in the arm. "Is this where you've been going after school all the time? To practice? Why didn't you tell me?"

"One—it's none of your business. And two—Penny asked me not to."

"How did this even happen?" I ask. Ben's always done his best to hide in his room whenever my friends were over. It wouldn't surprise me if he didn't even know their names!

He's still making a show of rubbing his arm, even though I'm sure I didn't hit him that hard. "I am a three-time winner of the talent show." I roll my eyes, but Ben ignores me. "So, when Penny decided she wanted to do it, her dads thought I might be able to give her some tips. Obviously, you already know she's a great singer. And I came up with the idea of accompanying her, which sounds better than singing to a recorded track."

Take a Breath Olive Tran

"And?" I ask.

"And what?" Ben replies.

"What do you get out of it?"

"Well...Peter may have agreed to give me driving lessons," he says with a grin. "You know how Mom always freaks out at the idea of me behind the wheel."

Before I can pepper him with more questions, Penny arrives and gets a giant hug from Peter and Neil. She peeks at me from the cocoon of her parents' arms.

"You were amazing, Penny," I say.

"Thanks," she says with a smile.

"Can I talk to you for a minute?" I ask.

"Olive, the Harrises are coming over for dessert," my mom tells me. "Why don't you two chat on the way home?"

88

Phuong Truong

"Okay. We'll be right behind you," I say. Once the others are far enough away that they can't eavesdrop, I turn to Penny. "I'm sorry things have been so weird between us. Is that why you didn't tell me you were going to do the talent show? Because you're mad at me?"

"Oh my gosh, no, I'm not mad at you!" Penny grabs my hand. "I was so nervous about the whole thing, I didn't tell anyone. I wanted to give myself an out in case I decided I couldn't go through with it. And you wanted us to get that pizza party so badly, I didn't want to get your hopes up. And then you started freaking out about the show, and I just went kablooey. I'm so sorry."

"Me too!" I cry and hug her hard. "I'm sorry my freaking out freaked *you* out. I

89

maybe need to speak a little less and listen a little more."

"No comment," Penny says with a small laugh. "I've been trying to talk to you about it all week, but we never seemed to be able to."

"Ugh, I've been practicing with the Chu Chums during lunchtime—"

"And I've been rushing home after school to practice with Ben," finishes Penny. "Are you mad at me for not telling you I'd signed up?"

"No! Well, maybe a little," I say. "I think I'm mostly disappointed. In myself for stressing out and making such a big deal of this party. And that we were in a place where you didn't feel you could talk to me."

Phuong Truong

Penny nudges me with her shoulder. "I think we can agree that we were both to blame for that."

"I guess I kinda went 'Olive' on the talent show, though, didn't I?"

"Yeah, that's kind of your thing," says Penny with a grin. It stings a bit, but I know she's not trying to be mean. And, if I'm completely honest with myself, she's right. Not everything has to be do or die. Make or break.

"Most importantly," I say as I pull Penny to a stop, "why have you been keeping your singing a secret? Not just from me, but from the world?"

Penny just shrugs. "I didn't know if I was any good. My dads have always told me I am, but they kinda have to say that."

Phuong Truong

"You are better than good. You are the best singer I've ever heard. No joke." I give her a tight squeeze. "And I think I know exactly what we need to do to get you the exposure you deserve...."

"Hey, did you hear about Ella's parents?" Penny asks quickly. I know she's trying to distract me, but she should know me better than that by now. "They said they would supply all the fixings for a sundae bar to go along with the pizza party!"

"That's amazing!" We're still holding hands, following behind our families, and about to have some dessert.

Pretty soon, our class is going to get to skip lessons in favor of a pizza party *and* an ice cream sundae bar. Just like I planned.

Best. Year. Ever.

About the Author

Phuong Truong grew up in Ottawa and dreamed of being a rock star, a lawyer, or a writer. She is pleasantly surprised to have achieved one of these goals. She is the author of *Everyone is Welcome* and the first book in the Olive Tran Series, *Every Little Bit Olive Tran*. She works in book publishing and lives with her family in Toronto, Ontario.

Get in touch with Phuong on Instagram!

@pt_author